P9-DHB-778

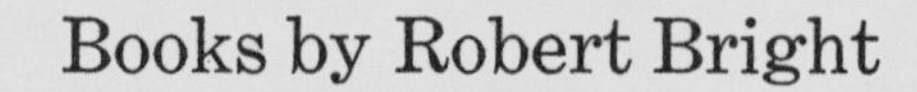

Books by Robert Bright

The Friendly Bear
Georgie
Georgie to the Rescue
Georgie and the Robbers
Georgie's Halloween
Hurrah for Freddie
I Like Red
Me and the Bears
Miss Pattie
My Hopping Bunny
Richard Brown and the Dragon
Which Is Willy?

Georgie to the Rescue

Written and illustrated by
ROBERT BRIGHT

Doubleday & Company, Inc.
Garden City, N. Y.

Library of Congress Catalog Card Number 56-5582.

ISBN: 0-385-07308-9 TRADE
ISBN: 0-385-07613-4 PREBOUND

15

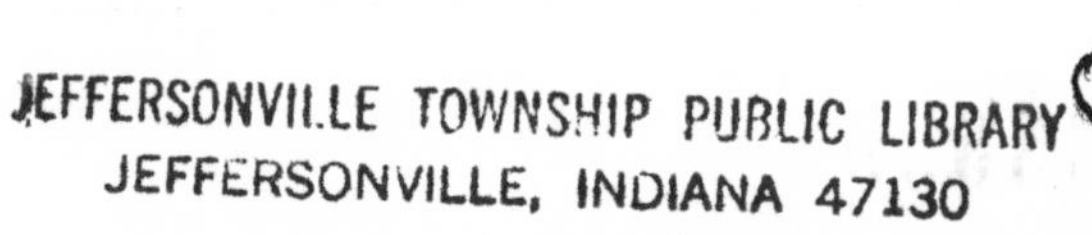

At the Whittaker house
in the quiet countryside
lived three staunch friends—
Herman the cat,
Miss Oliver the owl,
and Georgie
the gentle little ghost.

Every night Georgie would creak the stairs and squeak the parlor door,
and then Herman would prowl after his favorite mouse,
and Miss Oliver would waken and hoot in her favorite tree
while Mr. and Mrs. Whittaker would yawn and know it was time for bed.

So everything went peacefully and properly, until
one time Mr. and Mrs. Whittaker had a notion to visit the city.
They decided to take Herman along.

Miss Oliver could not imagine
Herman going without her
and left her favorite tree.

As for Georgie, who but he could make the little ghost sounds
that made everyone so comfortable!
So Georgie said good-by to his favorite attic.

They went by train
and that was all right.

And in the city
Mr. and Mrs. Whittaker took a room in a hotel
with a mouse for Herman.
And that was all right.

And while Miss Oliver
couldn't see a tree anywhere,
she found herself a perch
on a handy flagpole–
and that SEEMED all right.

But Georgie had to find
something to creak
and to squeak, of course.
The stairs wouldn't do.

The doors wouldn't do at all!

But the elevator
was quite satisfactory
because it was an old one
and clickered and clackered
and even wheezed a bit
the way Georgie ran it.

That was a lucky thing
because it made everybody
feel at home.
Mr. and Mrs. Whittaker
could sleep better.
Herman could prowl better

and Miss Oliver
could wake up properly
and say *whoo* on the flagpole,
just as she had always done
at home in her favorite tree.

Now everything would have been just as it should be
if it hadn't been for people noticing Miss Oliver
in the daytime while she was fast asleep.

It was the bellboy who saw her first.
He pointed her out to the doorman.
The doorman told the hotel manager.

The manager was very upset.
"This won't do at all," he said.
"What will the guests think?"
The hotel manager called a policeman.

The policeman called the firemen

and the firemen gave Miss Oliver to the zoo because she seemed such a rare bird for a city. Luckily Herman saw it all from his window.

He told Georgie as soon as it was dark.

Together, Georgie and Herman went to rescue Miss Oliver.

They took the bus.
It was quickest.
And they had the top
all to themselves.

When they got to the zoo
they knew at once
that they were in the right place.
Because they could hear whoooo

—and whooooo

–and WHOOOOO

And there was poor Miss Oliver in the rare-bird cage.

That was a fine how-do-you-do!

It would have been
very unfortunate except
that the night watchman
just happened to be about
with the key.

Georgie screwed up all
his courage
and said BOOOO!

The night watchman
was so astonished
at what he saw
in front of him
that he had no idea
what was going on behind him.

And so Georgie and Herman set Miss Oliver free

and then got right back to the hotel again

so that Georgie could clicker and clacker
and even wheeze the old elevator again.
And Mr. and Mrs. Whittaker
could sleep properly again
and Herman could prowl properly again.

But Miss Oliver
found herself a perch
where nobody,
NOBODY,
would bother her again

and went on sleeping—

until Georgie told her
that it was time to go back
to the country again.

And they all took
the train again
and got home
lickety-split—

thank goodness!